Curious George®

Builds a Home

Adaptation by Monica Perez
Based on the TV series teleplay written by Joe Fallon

Houghton Mifflin Harcourt Publishing Company
Boston   New York

For information about permission to reproduce selections from this book, write to Permissions, Houghton Mifflin Harcourt Publishing Company, 215 Park Avenue South, New York, New York 10003.

Library of Congress Cataloging-in-Publication Data is on file.

Design by Joyce White

www.hmhbooks.com

ISBN 978-0-547-59410-1
Manufactured in China
LEO 10 9 8 7 6 5 4 3 2 1
4500280259

It was a perfect day for sitting on the balcony, eating grapes, drinking juice, and drawing—all at the same time. George was a good little monkey who was good at many things. He was especially good at being curious.

Today George was curious about a bird. He had seen a lot of pigeons, but none wearing an ankle tag.

The pigeon had seen a lot of animals, but none drawing on a sketchpad. They spent the morning watching each other.

"George, this is your best drawing yet!" George's best friend, the man with the yellow hat, told him. "That tag the bird is wearing means that it is a homing pigeon. They're special birds that always return home."

George looked hopeful.
"Homing pigeons have special homes," the man added. "Our apartment is not a good home for a bird."

George saw that what his pigeon needed most was a place to roost.
A tree would be perfect. George came up with a great way to get a tree up
to his apartment. He would build one.

Uh-oh! The tree George built of pipe cleaners was not strong enough for a pigeon to sit on.

George thought of another idea. With clay, George could make a tree as big and thick as he wanted.

But George must have used too much water because the tree made of clay did not hold its shape.

George decided he needed more information to build the perfect tree, so he went to the park. He looked at the trees for a long time. He drew trees on a piece of paper.

Then he began a new project.

It took him a long time to build, but finally George revealed his masterpiece. It looked almost like a real tree. Baseball bats were the roots, and a coat rack was the trunk. A frayed brown rope was its bark.

Toilet paper and rubber gloves hung off it like leaves. George had even added real soil. George's friend the pigeon hopped onto a branch. He settled in.

That afternoon the man with the yellow hat brought home a guest. It was the doorman. He had lost one of his pigeons that he kept on the roof.

When they entered the apartment, they found . . . a big mess!

"George!" the man with the yellow hat exclaimed. "Is that—a tree?"
George nodded proudly. Now that he had the perfect home, the bird could
live with them forever.

But the doorman had missed his pigeon. When he called out, "Compass!" the happy bird flew right into his hands.

Poor George! He waved goodbye to Compass and the doorman. Then he sat alone on the balcony. The man with the yellow hat placed a potted tree on the ground. "I bought it for the birds to sit in so you can draw them," he said, trying to cheer George up.

George shook his head and pointed to his own tree.
The man said, "It was a good effort, George, but birds want to sit in a real tree."

But to George's delight, the birds did not agree with his friend. Not at all!

BUILD A HOME

George followed a series of logical steps in order to build his pigeon roost.
Engineers also use a similar process for technology design:

1. Start with a problem—state what needs to be designed or built.
2. Develop a design, or make a sketch, for solving the problem.
3. Build a model. If it works, great! If it doesn't, make changes to your design and try again. Be patient—it may take several tries.

Below are the steps George took in putting together his pigeon roost.
Study them and put them in the correct order.

_____

_____

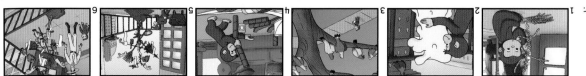

WHAT'S GEORGE UP TO?

Are you a good predictor? In the pictures below, can you guess what happens next?
Draw a line connecting the related images.